W9-BNQ-846

CRAZY like a FOX

A Simile Story

written and illustrated by Loreen Leedy

Holiday House • New York

What is a Simile?

A simile is a figure of speech used to compare two different things. It usually includes the words **like** or **as**. To say "Joe is **as** hungry **as** a bear" suggests that Joe's appetite is similar to a bear's (very big). To say "Rosa is growing **like** a weed" compares Rosa's growth rate to a weed's (very fast).

A simile may be an **idiom**, so its meaning isn't what the words actually say. If Tanisha has "a face like an open book," it doesn't mean she looks like a book. Instead, it means she shows her feelings easily.

Favorite similes may become popular **sayings** such as "It's as flat as a pancake" and "It's like taking candy from a baby." But a simile that is said too often may become a **cliché**, which means people are tired of hearing it. It's a good idea to learn the common similes and to be careful not to overuse them.

In the quiet forest, Rufus is sleeping like...

He's out like a light.

He's as snug as a bug in a rug.

He's as still as a stone.

When the sun comes up, he feels as fresh as...

Rufus will be as busy as a bee today.

I hope he's as fast as a shooting star.

...a daisy.

He looks as bright as a new penny.

He looks like a million bucks.

Rufus has a job to do,

so he zips across the meadow

as fast as...

He runs like a deer.

He's as quick as a wink!

...lightning.

Let's run like the wind!

He's like a bolt from the blue!

He's as cool as a cucumber.

She's as pretty as a picture.

He sneaks into Babette's yard like...

...a thief in the night.

He's as quiet as a mouse.

And as tricky as a box of monkeys.

Rufus tiptoes up behind her, takes a deep breath, and starts to roar like...

Babette is as innocent as a lamb.

Wow, you can fly like a bird!

My heart is beating like a drum!

RRRR!!!!!

Babette is so scared she starts to shake like...

... a hornet.

When she catches Rufus, he's going to cry like a baby.

Babette is as mad as a wet hen.

Babette grabs his tail, but he's as slippery as...

Rufus is as slick as a weasel.

And Babette is sticking like glue.

...a haystack.

It's as plain as the nose on your face.

This is like a bad dream.

He's as thin as a toothpick.

Suddenly a light shines as bright as...

Babette looks as happy as a pig in clover.

BIRTHDAY!

It's as noisy as a herd of...

She looks as happy as a clam.

SURPRISE!!!

She's like a kid in a candy store.

...elephants.

This party is like a three-ring circus!

I'm as hungry as a hippo.

This is like a day in the park!
Hey, Rufus, now I know why you were being so weird. To get me to the party, you acted crazy like...
I'm as hungry as a horse!

Your Simile Story

Most of the similes in this book are well known, but it's even more fun and creative to invent brand-new similes. If you want to say the weather is hot, think of very hot things such as a campfire, a volcano, or the surface of the sun. Maybe you would write, "The air feels like the burning breath of an angry dragon." Here are some simile starters to practice with:

As slimy as...? As useless as...? Messy like...? Amazing like...? As grumpy as...? As soft as...? Tough like...? As loud as...? Silly like...? As soft as...? Like eating...?

To create your own simile story, make a collection of similes you know or write new ones. Pick out your favorites and see how they might add up to a story. For example, "...cheeks like roses," "...as white as a ghost," and "...as green as grass" could be included in a story about colors. Or write a story first, then use familiar or original similes that fit into your story line. If you get as busy as a bee and work like a dog, it'll be as easy as pie to write your own simile story. Don't forget to draw illustrations too!

Some common sayings aren't factual. One example is "as blind as a bat," because bats really aren't blind. For more about similes, please visit www.loreenleedy.com.

It's as slimy as...

It's tough like...

Library of Congress Cataloging-in-Publication Data
Leedy, Loreen.
Crazy like a fox : a simile story / by Loreen Leedy.
p. cm.
Summary: In a story told entirely in similes,
Rufus the fox is behaving strangely, but for a very
good reason. Includes a definition of simile and suggestions
for writing a simile story.
ISBN 978-0-8234-1719-3 (hardcover)
[1. Surprise—Fiction. 2. Birthdays—Fiction.
3. Parties—Fiction. 4. Foxes—Fiction. 5. Animals—Fiction.
6. Simile—Fiction] I. Title.
PZ7.L51524Crd 2008
[E]—dc22
2007051016

...a worm in the rain?

...a rhino's hide?